A book is a treasure we keep in our memory chest...
this treasure belongs to:

_____

To My Beloved, Who Was The Light of Day

Published by Faux Paw Media Group, A Division of Faux Paw Productions, Inc.™

www.fauxpawproductions.com

Composed in the United States of America
Printed in China

First Impression 2006
ISBN 978-0-9777340-5-4
SAN: 850-637X

Library of Congress Cataloging-in-Publication Data

Carman, Debby
Cha Cha - The Dancing Dog / written and illustrated by Debby Carman

Summary: In rhyme, a dog who loves to dance just becuase it feels good.
(1. Dogs _ Fiction 2. Stories in Rhyme 3. Dance _ Fiction)
I. Title II. Carman, Debby

Cha Cha, The Dancing Dog

A parable written and illustrated
by Debby Carman©

Every now and again,
Not so often at all...

The oddest of tales gets chance to grow tall.

Her name is Cha Cha and not just by chance.
Her name is Cha Cha because she loves to dance!

Every now and again,
maybe once in
forNEVER,
A dog comes along
that does something
real clever.

Such is the story of
one remarkable dog,
once shaggy fur farce,
the "ulti·MUTT" dog.
Her name is Cha Cha
and not just by chance,
Her name is Cha Cha
because she loves to
DANCE!!

she's one fluffity puff,
spun like cotton candy...

With a bubble up spirit,
a loveable, danceable dandy!

But this little dog had one special gift,
A feeling of rhythm that gave her a lift!

In the middle of nothing,
from out of the blue...

Her paws begin tapping to an imaginary tune.

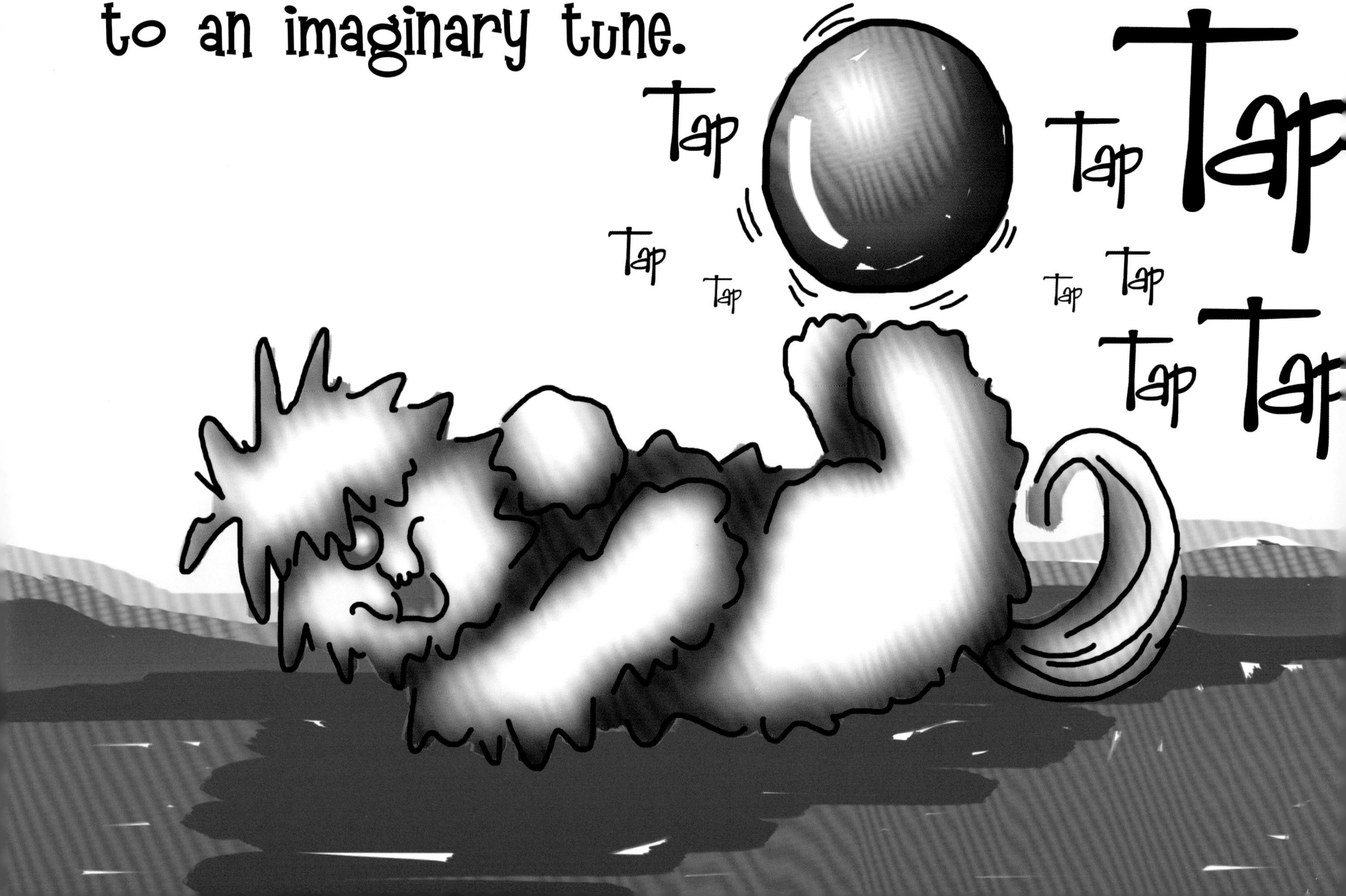

she begins to twist, then to shimmy and jiggle.

Twirling amongst the butterflies a-bobbin'.

when it's raining she dances
to the plip plop of the drops.

When it's sunny she soars,
spinning around without stops,

A dervishy whirl,
a flittery twirl...

Never sit the music out,
when you can be dancing about!!!

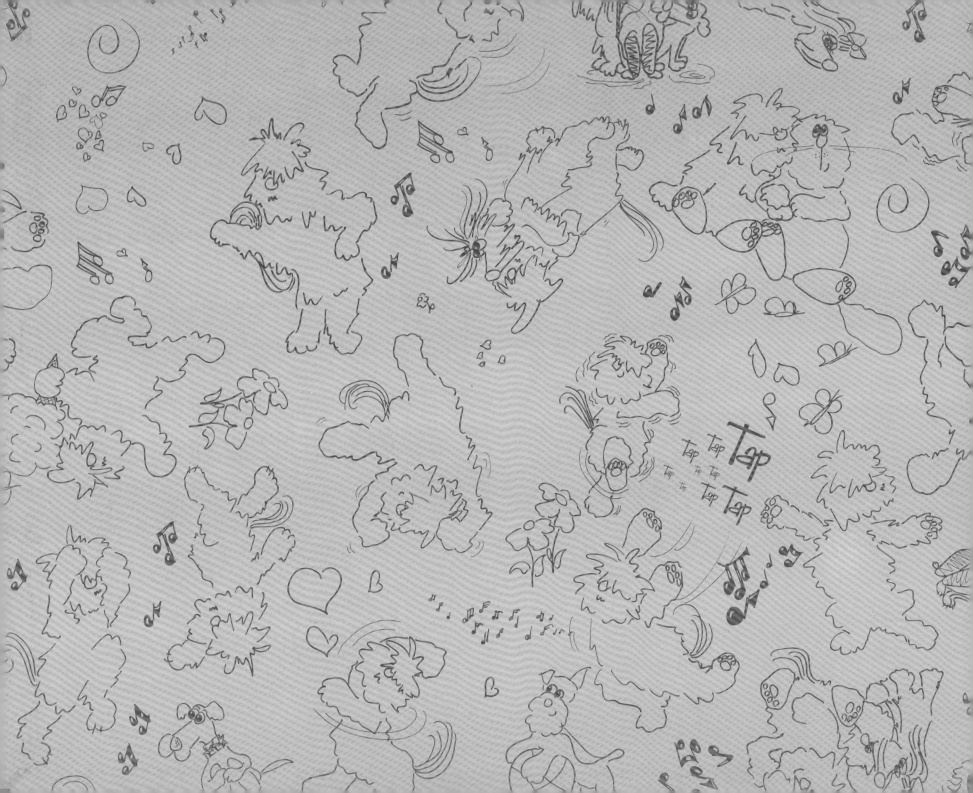